JEFFERSON

If you've already met *Chester* and *Eleanor* and the kids on the block—Jamie, Amy, Edie, George, and Zack—you're going to love *Jefferson*.

This time the problem is a simple birthday party for Chester's nice but jinxed brother Jefferson.

All the animals are here, too—Billybub the Dingo dog, King the piranha, Tui the goat, and, most of all, Zack's rat.

If you haven't met this great bunch of kids—meet them now.

Books by Mary Francis Shura

Jefferson
(a companion book to Chester and Eleanor)

Eleanor

Chester

Happles and Cinnamunger

The Barkley Street Six-pack

Mister Wolf and Me

The Gray Ghosts of Taylor Ridge

The Riddle of Raven's Gulch

Mary Francis Shura

JEFFERSON

ILLUSTRATED BY
Susan Swan

DODD, MEAD & COMPANY • NEW YORK

1   2   3   4   5   6   7   8   9   10

Library of Congress Cataloging in Publication Data

Shura, Mary Francis.
Jefferson.

Summary: All the neighborhood boys and girls work at
earning money to give Jefferson a surprise birthday party.
[1. Moneymaking projects—Fiction]   I. Swan, Susan
Elizabeth, ill.   II. Title.
PZ7.S55983Je   1984   [Fic]   83-27496
ISBN 0-396-08326-9

This book is for
Carrie Sprague
with all my love

Contents

Thursday

On that last Thursday before school let out, we decided to give Chester's brother Jefferson a surprise birthday party.

With as many kids as there are in our neighborhood, birthday parties happen all the time. I, Jamie, have very strong feelings about parties.

I like my own best because I get to keep the presents.

After that I like outdoor parties where you run a lot and sweat and eat all you want without somebody's mother following you around with a wet sponge.

Then there are those parties that make me sick. I start feeling queasy when the invitation comes. By the day of the party I am half dead. Mom just stiffens her back. "Party Pip," she diagnoses it. Her prescription is always the same—a clean shirt, dress pants, and out the door.

During that week in late May I discovered a whole new kind of party, one that you wish you'd never thought of, much less gotten into. You wouldn't think that one measly little birthday party for somebody's brother could ruin the whole end of the school year.

You would be wrong.

That Thursday was one really hot day. It always gets hot in the Millard C. Fillmore Elementary School District the last week of school. It may get hot all over town, for all I know, but I've always suspected that the weather is only trying to brace us for what's coming on grade card day.

That Thursday was the hottest day I can remember in my whole life. The neighborhood cats lay on their front porches pretending not to see birds walking on their lawns. The hill between school and home had stretched in the sun so that Chester's house, clear up at the top, looked about a million miles away.

We were all pushing our bikes toward home. You have to move your legs in a circle to pedal. It was all I could do just to lift one foot at a time and edge it forward. Even my socks were hot. They kept trying to crawl down into my tennis shoes to hide from the sun.

A stream was running down the middle of my back and making a lake at the top of my jeans. That always feels as if my brains are melting and I might have to think with the back of a soggy T-shirt.

Chester and I kept pushing our bikes along, listening to this big argument that George and Zach were having about how much school was left.

George, who is never a pussycat, turns to a real tiger when the weather gets hot. He claims to suffer more from the heat than the rest of us because he's all muscle. Personally I don't think that muscles gather at the front of your shirt and stick out. But since I'm that kind of kid who doesn't like to run for his life, I never mention the word "fat" to George.

"After all," Zach was saying, "we only have seventeen-and-a-half hours of school left this year. That's only one thousand and fifty minutes."

George frowned before he exploded. "Where did

you come up with that silly stuff? We have three whole days, Friday, Monday, and Tuesday, and then a half-day on Wednesday. If you take out lunch hours, that's still six hours a day. Twenty-one hours, that's what we have."

"Then it would be one thousand, two hundred and sixty minutes," Edie put in.

"Show-off," George barked at her. Only with a calculator could he ever have gotten that number so fast.

Zach shook his head. "We have two half-hour re-

cesses every day," he reminded George. "You can't count recess as school."

"I count recess," George told him. "I count recess because Mr. Allen is out there shouting at us and bouncing that ball every which way."

"With one hand," Amy added, which got her a glare from George. George is mad at our gym teacher because Mr. Allen chose that long-legged Abbie with the braces to be team captain the last month. When George used to be team captain, he thought Mr. Allen was the smartest man who ever wore racing stripes on his sweat suit.

Amy, who spends all her time trying to settle spats between her little brothers and sisters, tried to calm them. "In any case, school is almost over and we can settle down for a nice long summer."

"There are some really scary things about summer," Edie remarked thoughtfully. "Ants come out, and spiders. Snakes," she went on. Edie's like that. You mention anything in the world and she can find something dangerous about it.

"And bats," she added suddenly. "Bats fly around and get caught in your hair."

"Stop that," Amy ordered. "Everybody likes summer."

As I nodded agreement, I looked over at Chester. He didn't look as if he liked anything. He was plodding along with his head down and his freckles all wet and melted looking, like the chips in a cookie hot from the oven. He wasn't even smiling, and Chester always smiles.

Edie looked at Chester too. "What's the matter?" she asked.

"Jefferson," he said in a kind of basement tone of voice.

"Jefferson what?" George snapped.

"Jefferson is not a what," Chester replied, standing

14

up to George with a straight look. "Jefferson is a who. He's my brother."

Amy, our self-appointed referee, spoke up quickly. "Of course Jefferson is your brother, Chester. But which one is he?"

That stopped Chester for a moment. Chester has more brothers and sisters than anyone on our block (just as he has the most freckles and the most animals at his house and can run the fastest). He has more brothers and sisters than anyone in the Millard C. Fillmore Elementary School and maybe the world, for all I know.

There's Jefferson, whichever one he is. Then he has James and Franklin, and also Eleanor and Angela, and the twins. The twins are named Sam and Uel, because Chester's parents only had one name picked out but two kids came.

"Well," Chester was trying to explain, "Jefferson is after me and before James."

Edie was really trying. She was frowning as she asked, "Can't you just tell us what he looks like?"

Chester thought a minute. "He has sort of blondish hair that gets darker close to his head. He must have blue eyes because we all do. And he has freckles," Chester ended triumphantly.

I had to look the other way for fear Chester would see me swallowing a laugh. He had just perfectly described every single kid in his family. My mom once called them "peas in a pod." Considering how much I hate green things to eat, I took offense at that.

"Brussels sprouts in a bowl?" she'd asked then, grinning, to kid me.

"You must have some way you use to tell him from all those others," George said impatiently. He had stopped to wipe his face with the tail of his shirt, which was already wet from being pasted to his "muscles."

"He's bigger than James and smaller than I am," Chester said without thinking. Then, defensively, "I can tell my own brothers apart."

"So what's the matter with Jefferson?" Edie asked.

"Nothing," Chester said. "He's a perfectly nice brother. He does his share of the work and takes good care of Billybub, his dog. He's quiet and smiles a lot. At least, he used to smile a lot."

"Nobody smiles a lot when it's final-grade card time," Zach suggested. Zach is the best in the whole room in math but he still worries about grade cards. He holds the Millard C. Fillmore record for tardy marks. He really tries to be prompt, but by the time he finishes taking care of his animals, all the other kids are in their seats. He'll go to his grave not knowing what the tardy bell sounds like. It's always rung and been forgotten before he slides into the room, looking scared.

So far we've never heard of anyone being held back a grade for always being late, but Miss Button has written some pretty hysterical threats on the edge of his grade reports.

Chester shook his head. "Jefferson gets good enough grades. I don't think that's what's bothering him." Then, as if he just remembered, "His birthday's coming up next week."

"Aha," Amy cried. "That's it right there. He doesn't want to get any older and grow up. He probably dreads having to care for a family and having people hanging on him all the time."

Only Amy would have thought of that. But then, she's the only one who takes care of people and has them hanging on her all the time, and she isn't even grown up. She's the oldest of the Morris kids. The rest go down from her in a perfect alphabet. After Amy comes Bradford, then Carrie, then Douglas and Eliza and Franklin and last the baby, whom we only call G.

Mom says that Amy needs some genuine vanishing cream so she could watch those kids without their pawing her.

"Is your brother Jefferson going to have a party?" Edie asked.

Chester had a strange look on his face. "I guess not."

"Then that's the problem," Edie decided. "No wonder he is unhappy. I would be absolutely miserable if I couldn't have a party every single year. Once Mother thought I had a little fever and she canceled my party. It ruined my whole year. I just adore parties. Everyone does."

Zach and I exchanged a long meaningful look. Edie has just the kind of party that your mother makes you go to even if you have held the thermometer under hot water and raised it five degrees.

Just thinking about Edie's parties makes me feel queasy. You really have to dress up for them. "It won't hurt you to behave like a gentleman for one afternoon," Mom says. A lot Mom knows about how a gentleman feels. Did she ever sit in a chair with her feet dangling until both legs went to sleep? One year I had such pins and needles when we got up for Musical Chairs that my legs turned to rubber. I fell right into a bowl of raspberry punch. I thought I might not be invited again, but no such luck.

Even the cake isn't worth the trip. They serve it in little squares that Mom calls "dainty." I say that if I can put a whole piece of cake in my mouth and say "Thank you" without spitting crumbs, it's not cake at all but a damp cookie.

"Maybe your mother's too busy to give a party,"

Edie suggested. "Could all of us get together and surprise your brother Jefferson on his birthday?"

"Yeah," George said, looking a little more alive. "We could hold the party in the park and have races and win prizes."

I glared at George. All he thinks about is racing and winning. Until Chester came, nobody ever beat George in a race. But that first day that Chester was there, someone asked him why he wore a green sock on his left foot. Chester explained that he was left-footed and he did that to remind himself that his left foot was his "Go" foot. Then Chester got off to a winning start while George was still trying to figure out whether he was left- or right-footed. George still thinks it's an accident every time he gets beaten.

"Jefferson's not much for racing," Chester said. "He likes other things."

"What other things?" Zach asked. Zach likes animals better than anything else. His pets take up all his spare time. Since he is going to be a veterinarian, he practices on his dogs and cats, mice, gerbils, guinea pigs, two canaries, and a rat. He's saving up now for a wombat.

Zach's question threw Chester for a loss. I wondered if Chester's brains were melting and running down his back, too. "He's really crazy about that Billybub, that dingo dog of his," he said finally. "And other things," he finished, kind of limply.

"We could play Musical Chairs," Edie said brightly.

At the very mention of that game I could feel the raspberry punch dripping off my chin onto my Sunday shirt.

George scoffed. "Boys don't like games like that."

Edie glared at him and was puffing up to tell him off when Chester spoke up again.

"Anyway, we can't have a party because we already voted all our funds away."

I guess we all stared at him. "Funds?" I asked.

He nodded. "There are such a bunch of us, it takes a lot to raise us. When there is extra money, we put it into a fund. Then we all vote on how we want to use it. Everyone but Sam and Uel vote, that is. Sometimes we vote to take a trip. This year we all agreed on sending Eleanor away to camp."

I stopped so fast that Amy ran into me and skinned the back of my ankle with her bike. "Eleanor to camp?" I asked. Summer vacation was still hazy in my mind, but I knew I wanted Eleanor to be a part of it. Eleanor is Chester's older sister. She's excellent, that's what Eleanor is—excellent.

She looks like Chester but somehow a lot better. She has a way of smiling that stretches you up taller than those trick mirrors in the fun house.

"Yeah." Chester really smiled then. "She's going off

to camp and have a wonderful time. And write us cards every week."

"Why do you need money for a party?" Edie asked.

George scoffed again. "Prizes, silly."

"And food and balloons and ice," Zach added.

"Cake doesn't grow on trees," Amy told her. "Or paper napkins or ice cream."

I was glad Edie had asked first. I'd never thought about the money. Mostly Mom complains about the mess and not being able to play tennis all week because she is "throwing a party."

"We could raise money," I suggested. "Didn't you say his birthday isn't until next week?"

"The last day of school," Chester told me.

"What rotten luck," Zach groaned. "Imagine getting a year older on top of your grade card."

"That's a *perfect* day," Edie said. "We only have school half a day and there's that whole afternoon left."

We had almost reached Amy's house. It was clear what she was in for. Her brothers and sisters were lined up in the window in matching yellow-and-black striped bathing suits. The girls' hair was fastened up. They all had towels over their arms and the sprinkler was ready to be plugged in out on the lawn.

At the sight of her turning in, they disappeared from the window and started spilling out the front door like so many little hornets in for the kill.

"You can count on me," Amy shouted above the screeching of all those little voices.

"And me," Zach called, edging through his gate so that the puppies hurling themselves against it wouldn't fly out into the street.

Edie's mother was at the window making frantic motions for her to come inside.

"You know you can depend on me," Edie said, starting up the walk. By the time she was halfway to the house, her mother was at the door and calling.

"Don't run, dear. Take your time. You'll have a heatstroke for sure."

George's mother already had their sprinkler running.

George let out this big yelp and ran to stand right in the middle of it in his school clothes and everything. It was coming down on top of his head. He caught it running off his face with his tongue like an anteater with a nest of termites in its hair.

"That sure is a great bunch of kids," Chester said.

"Sure we are," I agreed. "You don't sound very happy about the party idea, though."

"Well . . ." Chester hesitated. "If it was anybody but Jefferson, I might be."

"What's the matter with Jefferson?" I asked.

The minute the words were out I knew I was wasting them. Mom says she never saw a family so loyal. Not one of those kids ever says anything bad about another one, even if it's true. That's a nice trait all right, but it sure keeps you from being prepared for what's coming.

"Nothing's the matter with Jefferson," Chester said. "After all, he's my brother." Then he hesitated. "Do you understand magnets?"

I hesitated. As sure as I said I did, he would ask me to explain them. I'm that kind of kid who hates trying to explain things he doesn't understand. "I know how they work," I told him.

"Well," he said slowly. "If trouble were a metal, then Jefferson would be a magnet."

"You mean he's a jinx," I suggested.

Chester sighed. "I don't like name-calling."

"There's a difference between name-calling and making a definition," I told him.

He nodded. "Okay. Then you could define Jefferson as a person who attracts trouble the way a magnet does a pin."

I might have asked him for particulars about that but someone was coming up the hill and calling to us.

Eleanor.

She was wearing a yellow hair ribbon to hold back her hair. Her blouse was the color of butter and didn't have even one sweat spot on it.

"Hi, fellows," she said, standing over her bike and smiling at us. "I'm glad I caught you, Jamie. I wanted to wish you a happy summer before I went off to camp."

There's a little weed in our yard with leaves almost like a clover. It blooms with tiny little peaky blossoms. When you bite the leaves, they taste sweet and really sour at the same time. Eleanor's words hit me like that. It's really nice when someone wishes you a happy summer. It's really horrible when they tell you good-bye in the very same breath.

Chester was looking at his sister and not smiling.

"What's the matter, Chester?" she asked, a sudden little line between her eyebrows.

"The kids are talking about having a surprise party for Jefferson," he told her.

She didn't say anything for a minute. She just looked at Chester soberly. Then she turned to me.

"Did Chester tell you about Jefferson?" she asked.

I almost said the word "jinx" before I realized it would sound as if Chester had been calling him names. "A little bit," I replied.

She stared at me then and smiled that slow way that makes me not want her to go away even as far as the corner, much less all summer to camp.

"I do admire courage," she said softly. "Courage is something I really do admire."

She was back on her bike and starting up the hill. "Goodbye again, Jamie," she called back. "And good luck. Really good luck!"

Friday

Mom somehow has summer vacation confused in her mind with Death Row.

From about the middle of May on, she starts announcing "last things" she is doing. "Today is my last day to have lunch downtown with the girls." "Today is the last bridge luncheon." Stuff like that.

That Friday she was cooking breakfast with a huge apron tied over her tennis clothes. She was trotting back and forth with only bare legs and tennis shoes showing from under that thing. She looked like one of those plastic dolls that walk by themselves down a slanted board.

"That's an interesting costume," Dad commented, peering over the sports section, which he calls the "gentleman's page."

"It looks really nice underneath," she told him. "I

have on my very best tennis dress. We're all having lunch after tennis. It's the last day, you know."

"The condemned mother played a hearty three sets," I said.

Right away I was sorry. I needed her help in getting the party together, and that was no way to line up the troops.

Dad chuckled. "That's right. This is the last week before school lets out, isn't it? How are you figuring to spend your summer, Jamie?"

I was careful to keep my eyes on my plate. "Mowing the lawn, keeping my room tidy, helping Mom around the house, letting things alone that I have no business fooling with."

Sheer exaggeration always breaks Mom up. Her coffee made little waves in her cup.

"The very first afternoon we are giving a birthday party for Jefferson," I went on, jumping right in while she was still smiling.

"Not here," she said swiftly. She hadn't been as amused as I thought.

Dad gave up on the paper and folded it by his plate. "Now wait, honey," he told Mom. "Who is this Jefferson?"

"He's Chester's brother," I answered. "And Eleanor's." My folks really like Chester but they admire Eleanor.

"Then they can have the party at Chester and Elea-nor's house," Mom announced firmly.

I shook my head. "It's a surprise party. You can't surprise anyone in his own house."

"We could have a whole discussion on that thought," Mom said. "But this party is not going to be at our house."

"You're awfully sensitive about this," Dad told her, his tone a little confused.

"The birthday-party fund in this house is only slightly smaller than the mortgage payment," she told him icily. "This is the only neighborhood in the world where a mother has to buy wrapping paper with can-dles on it in gross lots. I give Jamie one party a year. Then I buy a three-dollar present for Amy's party, for Zach's party, for George's party, and Edie's party. By that time we've worked through the year and are start-ing again."

"George suggested that we have the party in the park," I told her. "But could you just give me the three dollars instead of buying a present?"

"You can pick out a three-dollar present," she told me.

"We have all this stuff we need to buy—food and prizes and balloons. We plan to raise enough money, but it would be nice to know I had three dollars to fall back on."

Mom has this theory that the only place a parent is safe is way ahead of its child. She was clearly working on this thought.

"We are not zoned for business at this house," she reminded me. "How do you propose to raise all this money somewhere else?"

Dad saved me by looking at the clock and getting up.

"What time were you due for tennis?" he asked her.

She squeaked to her feet and started clearing the table into the sink.

Like I said, I'm that kind of kid who hates being asked questions he doesn't know how to answer.

George prides himself on knowing all the answers.

"We start with the easy money first," he announced as we were all going down the hill toward school.

Not knowing what easy money was, we just waited.

"People drop money all the time," he explained. "We just go and pick it up."

When Zach hooted, George flushed. "At the same time we can collect bottles and cans to sell."

"I know I won't be allowed to do that without even asking," Edie told us. "Traipsing around town could get you run over by a car. Then there are downtown diseases that you'd never catch out in a neighborhood."

Amy glared at her but looked doubtful. "It won't be easy to trail all those kids around behind me. Especially not in this heat."

Zach gave her a horrified look. "That would be awful for you," he agreed. He didn't add that it wouldn't be any picnic for the rest of us. I wouldn't say that the Morris kids have short spans of attention but they remember the word "behave" about two-and-a-half minutes at a time.

"Anyway," Zach went on. "Somebody needs to make up a list of other ways for us to make money."

Amy rose to that instantly. "I'll do that. And, Edie, you can surely think of some party thing to do."

"Place cards," Edie said happily. "I could make a place card for everybody and print the names on with a picture."

"For a picnic?" George scoffed.

Edie glared at him. "I'll think of something. And you just try to find out what it is before the actual day of the party. Just try!"

Chester shook his head. "I wish I could go along and help but I promised Mom I'd do a job for her this afternoon. But I'll help tomorrow for sure."

After school Zach had to take care of his animals so George and I each had a snack while we waited for him. The condemned mother had apparently played

30

well. She had smeared some white stuff on her nose. Instead of giving me just four cookies, she filled a plate with cookies and sat down with me.

"Who is Jefferson again?" she asked.

"Chester and Eleanor's brother."

"I guess I don't know him from the others. What's he like?" she asked.

"Nobody seems to know," I admitted.

She took the empty plate and grinned at me. "Well, speaking as 'your father's wife' and 'Jamie's mother,' I know the feeling. I also used to be 'somebody's sister' and that wasn't much fun, either."

"Uncle Dan's sister?" I guessed.

At her nod I told her what a nice brother she had.

"He has a pretty nice sister too—whatever her name is." Then she smiled, looking back at me from the sink.

"In the last resort—I mean the *very* last resort—if you need help for this brother's picnic, whistle."

Although that Friday afternoon wasn't as hot as Thursday, it was bad enough to make me wish the park pool would open before Memorial Day. George brought a sack for cans and Zach brought one for bottles. Zach had changed into a light-blue cotton shirt. I remembered that shirt because he once told me it was the same shade as the eyes of the white rat that mostly rides around in his shirt pocket.

First the three of us checked bus stops because people don't like poking in snowdrifts for dropped dimes when their bus is bearing down. But the snow had been gone too long. After seven bus stops, we only had two dimes and a bent penny.

The seventh bus stop was on a corner. There by the curb was a grating for the water to run down into.

Zach squatted to peer through the grating.

"I bet there's money down there," he said. "But I can only see leaves and grass and some broken glass."

"Maybe we should stir it around to see," I suggested.

George got a crooked stick and tried to stir the mess down there. Mostly stuff just hooked onto his stick.

"That grate doesn't look so heavy." George said. "And it's not bolted down or anything."

Famous last words, I think you call those.

We hooked our fingers in and tugged until the grate shifted. We tried again. It must have been stuck because when it let loose it came fast, popped out of the frame, and landed on George's foot.

George grabbed his foot and started yelling bloody murder and jumping around. Zach watched him a minute and then slid down into the hole.

Scratch a veterinarian and you get a scientist. Zach was all bent over, poking around.

"Rats have been down here," he called up as if that were some big treat.

"Rats," George yelped, forgetting his foot to lean over and look. "There are rats down there?"

"Now now," Zach said comfortably. "But they've been here."

"Yuck," George commented, hanging onto his foot again.

Zach found a quarter, three nickles, and seven pennies before he quit scruffing that stuff around. I was trying to tug him back up when somebody spoke behind us.

We have a really nice police officer who patrols over by the Millard C. Fillmore Elementary. He's tall and skinny and likes kids and smiles a lot. This was a different one in every way.

"What do you kids think you're doing?" he asked.

Zach grinned up from down in that hole.

"Looking for something lost," he replied. "But I've got it now."

"Well, okay." The policeman softened a little. "Get up out of there and let's shut this thing up."

George and I both pulled on Zach but he's heavier than he looks. The policeman glared and carefully got down on his knees to give it a try.

I thought maybe I was the only one who heard that

funny little tearing sound. But when Zach was up, the policeman reached around and felt the back of his trousers. Now he was scowling.

I never saw anybody stand so straight and try to put a grating back in. When people walked up or cars passed, the police officer turned this way and that to keep his front toward them.

The grate didn't go back in any easier than it had come out. "Now," he said, when finally he had it wedged in place. "Don't you kids ever try that trick again on my beat."

Then he frowned. "School isn't out already, is it?"

"Not until next Wednesday," I told him. "Thanks a lot. We really appreciate your help."

"Sure," he said. "Sure," as if he were thinking of something else. "A long hot summer," he muttered to himself. "I have the feeling this will be a long hot summer."

"Forty-seven cents," George said triumphantly as if he had been down there scruffing in that rathole. "Forty-seven cents and we've hardly started."

I had seven aluminum cans in my sack and Zach had three bottles in his. The policeman was still walking off down the street like a crab, going sideways to keep his back away from the street.

George suggested parking meters next. We walked about ten blocks and didn't find so much as a penny.

We were passing the laundromat on High Street. You could smell washing powders clear out on the sidewalk.

"All those machines work with coins," George said. "Let's try them."

It was really hot and noisy in there. The washers sloshed and gurgled. The dryers either marched or clinked, depending on whether it was tennis shoes or belts tumbling around in them. I was so busy poking around the bottoms of the change machines that I didn't see the kid standing there right off. Zach did.

"Hi," Zach said. "Don't I know you?"

"Yeah," the boy replied. "I'm Chester's brother."

Chester and I saw each other at the same instant. He was pulling stuff out of a dryer into a rolling basket.

"What's going on?" I asked him.

"The washing," Chester explained. He waved his hand at about ten machines, all of them spinning soap and water like crazy.

"All of them are yours?" I asked.

He nodded. "This was Eleanor's idea. It used to take all day to do our washing with just one machine at home. And then when we hung it up, Tui always ate off the bottom half of everything."

All of us like to hear about Tui. George and Zach came up grinning. Tui is the goat that belongs to Chester's family. She isn't what you'd call beautiful but she's something special. She probably saved all our lives once by chasing a bad driver off the road. Then another time she saved the honor of the whole Millard C. Fillmore School on field day.

"Tui ate what?" George asked.

"Everything she could reach by standing on her hind legs," Chester told him. "That's Jefferson over there, helping me."

We all turned to stare at the boy by the change machines. I was looking for something different enough to remember. He looked smaller than Chester. He was probably bigger than James, but without James there to compare them, that didn't help.

George's voice fell to a whisper. "Look what we got already. Show him, Zach."

Zach fished in his jeans pocket and pulled out all the money to show Chester.

"Hey," Chester said. "That's great."

Then, as Zach was closing his hand on the money, Chester let out a yelp.

"Let me see that dime again." He took a coin out of Zach's hand and examined it close up. "This isn't just any ordinary dime," he told us. "This is a real silver dime. See that date on there? It says 1956. This is worth more because it's made of real silver."

We all had to look.

"Maybe we could sell it," Zach suggested.

George nodded. "There's a shop in the train station where they buy silver."

I looked at Jefferson one more time as we left. He was loading dryers and stuffing quarters into their slots. Even his freckles were arranged on his face the way Chester's are. Anybody could tell he was Chester's brother, but who could possibly tell that he was Jefferson?

Zach put our money in the pocket of that blue shirt and we went to the train station.

The man in the coin shop had a customer with an Indian head penny. He was staring at the penny through a little spyglass that hung down in front of one eye. When the man with the Indian head penny left, it was our turn.

"We have a real genuine silver dime," George announced. "How much will you give us for that?"

"That would depend on a lot of things," the man with the glass replied. "What year is it?"

"Nineteen fifty-six," George told him.

The man nodded. "If it is a proof coin, it is worth two dollars. Otherwise, it is worth fifty or fifty-five cents, depending on its condition."

George whistled softly. "Give him the dime, Zach," he ordered.

Zach reached into his pocket and brought out the

money. He had all eight of the pennies, the quarter, and the three nickels, but no dimes at all. He looked funny and started feeling in his pocket again.

"You lost it," George said, his voice awfully loud in that little tiny shop. "You lost our silver dime."

"But it was right here," Zach said, trying to see down into his own shirt pocket.

George leaned over and put his hand in Zach's pocket. His finger came right through the bottom and waggled.

"Big mystery," he scoffed. "You lost our money through that hole in your pocket."

Zach looked really sick. "My rat," he said quietly to himself.

Then I remembered. I remembered the day he was carrying his rat in that shirt because it matched the rat's eyes. The tail of the rat had hung down from the pocket on top of the shirt.

"This is my own invention," Zach had told me. "It hurts him to fold his tail up, so I made him a tail hole."

George was beginning to yell and the man asked us to leave.

By the time we got to our street, George was too mad even to yell any more. And his foot had gotten a lot worse. He was hobbling along and glaring at Zach with every step.

When we got to Zach's house, Zach handed me the

coins that were left. There was only that bent penny from the bus stop and the forty-seven cents from the grating. Both dimes were gone.

"I'm really sorry," he told me. "Maybe I should back out of the whole thing after what I did."

"Back out!" George exploded. "After you lose all our money, you back out?"

"Who found the money?" Zach challenged him. "So I had a little bad luck."

"Rathole," George yelled at him. "Two dollars right down a rathole."

"Probably only fifty or fifty-five cents," Zach corrected him.

George was even hopping on his sore foot. The two of them probably would have fought if Chester's mother hadn't driven down the street in their truck and we all started waving at Eleanor, beside her in the seat.

George had his fists still balled and was starting to shout, but Zach's pups set up such a lot of welcome barking that you could barely make out what he was saying.

"That's it," George screamed. "I'm the one that's backing out. I don't deal with ratholes like you."

He limped off and we watched him.

"What's more," he shouted from his front door. "Mom offered to supply cold drinks for the whole party. Now you can just go thirsty. Rathole!"

Zach sighed. "I really am sorry, Jamie."

"It was just bad luck," I told him. "Amy says that tomorrow we are going to have a car wash. There's always money down under the seats of cars, and people will pay a whole dollar for the washing."

He ducked his head and went inside to feed his animals.

I had forgotten about money under seats until it came right out of my mouth. I went through the chairs at home. I found a yellow comb with a tail, two tiles from my Scrabble game, two dimes, and a lot of pencil stubs. There were also a lot of pieces of dusty-looking popcorn.

Chester was yelling from outside.

"Eleanor's putting the clothes away," he told me. "How much did you get for the silver dime?"

When I told him the story, he listened with a strange look on his face.

"Once our family saved paper bingos for a grocery store game. We had all the winners to get a hundred dollars. Then one of the kids popped the B into his mouth and swallowed it."

"A hundred dollars," I echoed.

He grinned. "We laugh about inow but it wasn't funny then."

Then it struck me.

"One of the kids?" I asked.

"One of my brothers," he replied, looking at me that straight way.

"Jefferson?" I guessed out loud.

"Jefferson," he said, turning to go back uphill.

Saturday

You have to give Amy credit. She really jumps into things. By the time George and Zach and I got back that Friday afternoon with our forty-eight cents, she had come up with a money-making idea for every single day. Jefferson's party was looking better and better, all jinxes aside, of course.

The man down at the corner in the house with the cottonwood tree had sold the house and was moving away. He had posted signs for a garage sale on Sunday. Amy had already talked him into letting us put some toys in with his things to sell before she even asked us to collect them.

Saturday morning while I cleaned my room, I tried hard to forget about the party and Jefferson. You'd think it would be easy not to worry about a kid you can't even recognize except by comparison, but it wasn't.

Jinx is that kind of word that makes me want to look back over my shoulder to see if anybody is behind me.

Not thinking about Jefferson took so much energy that I didn't do the world's best job of cleaning my room. I didn't realize that it was the world's worst job until Mom came in to check on it.

She threw my closet open with her old flourish. That was her first mistake. Her second mistake was not jumping back fast.

All the stuff I had balanced up there on the closet shelf came down at once. Instead of raining cats and dogs, she got baseballs and those little rubber astronauts.

She stood there a minute with a jumping rope over her shoulder, buried to the knees in frisbees and balls. That old orange hula hoop had made a perfect ringer of her head and shimmied straight down to her ankles. I didn't dare laugh but it was really like a cartoon. Into that silence came a few notes on a tambourine beaten by a wind-up monkey that got his arms jarred loose in the fall.

She didn't say anything. She didn't need to. I'm that kind of a kid who can read columns in the way a woman stamps back downstairs.

I looked at all that stuff on the floor. It wouldn't fit into anything but the orange crate I had been saving since Christmas. The trouble was, there wasn't room anyplace for the orange crate. That's how I selected what I would take to the garage sale. Everything fitted in but the hula hoop which I laid on top.

When I was scraping the last of the fallen jacks out from under the bed, my hand hit something fuzzy. I'm no Zach. I not only don't want to be where rats have been, I don't want to be where rats are.

When I pulled up the cover to stare back in there, I saw it had a claw and I remembered losing my rabbit foot. It was on a chain and read "Souvenir of Cheyenne, Wyo." in faded letters on a little tag.

I almost threw it into the crate too before I remembered and put it in my jeans pocket. I hate to sound like Edie but, for all I know, being a jinx could be catching. And Eleanor had wished me good luck, not once but twice.

"So how are you kids going to earn all this money?" Mom asked when I got her approval on my room (third try).

"Amy's got it organized," I explained. "She's good at organizing things."

45

Amy had been captain of the Great Goat Hunt the time Chester's goat, Tui, walked away and disappeared. In the end Tui found us, but Amy sure had us organized while we weren't finding her.

"No wonder she's organized," Mom said. "A three-ring circus looks easy next to those little clowns of hers." She poured a cup of coffee and sat down with me. "This idea of the toy sale is going to be a help at this house."

"Then we're going to have a car wash."

"Where?" She shot up straight that way she does.

"Got you," I grinned. "Right in people's own driveways."

"Then Zach is going to guess how many jelly beans there are in that fishbowl in the window of Prescott's Five and Dime."

"Oh, Jamie," she said. "Prescott has been offering ten dollars for the right answer ever since I can remember. Those jelly beans are so dusty that the whole top layer looks like grape. I know a few children up on their feet walking who are younger than those jelly beans."

"Never mind," I told her. "Zach has a surefire plan."

With a thud I realized that Zach had thought the "found money" idea was surefire too.

As I left, Mom was looking at me thoughtfully.

"Would you still like that three dollars instead of buying a present?"

I remembered the silver dime that had escaped through the rathole in Zach's shirt and hesitated.

"Can we just wait and see?" I asked.

We went to pick up George but he wouldn't even come outside. He shouted at us over the Saturday morning cartoons on TV.

"No way," he told us. "I should knock myself out and get a crippled foot for somebody I don't even know? Let Rathole Zach help you wash cars."

"Wash cars," Edie's mother squealed when we rang the Danvers' bell. "Jamie, what are you thinking of? With only a few days of school left, you could catch colds and miss it all."

"But it's seventy-seven degrees out here," I told her. "How could we catch a cold from all this hot?"

"Summer colds are the worst kind," she declared in that final tone. "Edie wants to do her part for this child . . ." She paused. "What's his name again?"

"Jefferson," I said.

"And who is he?"

"He's Chester and Eleanor's brother."

"We'll make sandwiches for the party," she told us. "And Edie has made this beautiful sign, but she can't wash cars."

The sign was beautiful. Edie's really good with stuff like that. This one said $100. CAR WASH in letters about a foot high.

"Isn't that a little expensive?" I asked.

Edie looked at it and changed the period so that it read one dollar instead of a hundred dollars. Edie's a lot better at printing than she is at punctuation.

"What about Amy?" Zach shouted over his puppies when Chester and I stopped there.

"Maybe her kids will keep her in," Chester suggested. Instead she came out the front door with her hair tied up and a bucket and sponge in her hand.

"Got any customers yet?" she asked. "I promised Bradford a trip to the park if he watched them during the cartoons."

We started at the top of the block up by Chester's and knocked on every door.

The lady in the first house was gone for the day and had taken her car with her.

The man across the street told us that the only exercise he ever got was washing his car but thanks anyway.

By the time we were turned down by the woman with the apple tree next door to us, I was getting discouraged.

"We could ask your mom," Amy suggested.

"Only as a last resort," I told her. I didn't want to

take any chances with that three dollars.

Finally we got a customer and Amy's idea began to look a lot better.

We washed a blue car for the man next door to Edie's. Either he didn't trust us or he was lonesome. He stayed outside and watched us the whole time.

He and Zach got into a conversation about whether turtle wax really came from turtles and, if so, what kind of turtles. As a consequence, Amy and Chester and I did most of the work.

The man quit talking to Zach when we told him we were through and asked to be paid. He walked around his car and found about seventeen smudges and a mud streak. There hadn't been any money in under the seat but, when he finally said he guessed it was okay, he gave us half a dollar as a tip. That's a lot of dimes.

When we rang the doorbell on the next house, the man came out, looked at us, and laughed.

"Are you kids serious?" he asked.

When we told him we were trying to make money to give a surprise party, he fished around in his pocket and handed us a dollar. "Just let me make a donation and forget about the car."

Chester hesitated. "That doesn't seem fair. Don't you even want a quick wash?"

The man looked up the street to where the blue car

was sitting out in the sun developing cloudy-looking places here and there.

"Let's say that is my payment for your *not* washing it," he told us. "And wish your brother a happy birthday."

We all took a break for lunch after that. We had all come out but Amy as we went on to the last house down by the corner. The woman who lives there is really old. Her car looks like the ones in black-and-white movies. She has the nicest flowers on the block in her back garden. She has a birdbath with a fish sticking up in the middle and, back under the trees, some beehives on little stools. All of this behind a high fence that you can hardly see through.

Mom says that both the flowers and the fence represent the wisdom of age. With all those bees back there, that woman doesn't really need a fence, even though she does have great-looking strawberries.

The woman thought a long time before she decided that we could wash her car for a dollar. We waited while she got her keys and backed her car out into the driveway. By then Amy was coming with Bradford and Carrie trailing behind her.

"Who are all those children?" the woman asked, looking over the part of her glasses that was thickest.

"The Morris kids," Zach told her.

"All of them?" Her voice was threatening to squeak.

Amy was there by then, smiling up through her bangs. "Oh, my, no," she told the woman. "The little ones are down for naps. Bradford and Carrie are going to sit on the curb and watch. Aren't you, Bradford and Carrie?" she asked, a little louder and grinning that way that shows all her teeth.

Both kids nodded more times than they needed to.

We had the car all soaped up by the time Douglas started toward us across the street. Amy sat him down with the others and whispered something that stiffened their backs for a while.

This car was really easy to wash. A little shelf ran along the side just below the doors. Amy could stand on that on tiptoe and scrub the whole top of the car.

Chester had turned the hose on to rinse it when Amy looked over to see only two kids sitting there.

"Douglas," she shouted. "Where's Douglas?"

We all looked around for him. Then Chester dropped the hose and ran straight for the fence, shouting, "No, Douglas. NO!"

Through the fence, we could see Douglas clear at the back of the woman's yard. He had a stick in his hand and he was walking toward that square box where the bees live.

I never thought I'd ever see Chester tackle anything he couldn't do. But he couldn't climb that fence. Either the holes in the wire were too small or his tennis

51

shoes were too big, I don't know which. He was half-way up and still falling back when Douglas put the stick under that box and flipped it off its stool.

I couldn't move.

Do you remember the story about Aladdin and his wonderful lamp? Remember the scene where he rubs his lamp and this cloud rises up, bigger and bigger, until it fills the sky above him? Later the smoke clears and you can see the face of the genie looking out at Aladdin.

Douglas had everything but the smiling face of the genie. That cloud of bees rose and swirled and seemed to fill the sky. You could hear them hum from clear out there in the driveway.

In the story, the genie asks Aladdin what he wants.

Those bees knew what they wanted, and it was Douglas.

We only found out how he got in there when he came flying out. There was a door at the back of the garage and Douglas raised smoke on that cinder path getting to it.

The only problem was that he ran straight for us, bringing his bees with him.

I don't know who got bitten first, but one got Amy on the arm. She slapped at it with the sponge and lost her balance and slid right down the windshield of that car.

Chester grabbed the hose and was hosing off every-body as soon as the bees hit.

The woman at the door was screaming, "Go home! Go home! All of you go *home*!"

She didn't have to tell me that many times.

Well, it was all over but the counting. I had seven bee stings. Chester had eleven. Amy had fourteen, most of them around her face. Zach only had three. Bradford and Carrie had run straight home and didn't get a one.

By all rights, Douglas should have been stung more than any of us. Instead he had run fast enough to beat the bees. Once he got out where Chester could turn the hose on him, the bees were washed off before they could sting. Talk about life being unfair.

What you do for a lot of bee stings is call the doctor.

Mom was yelling into the telephone at Dr. Goodson, literally screeching, which isn't her normal style. Dad kept smearing a paste of soda and water on me while she carried on to the doctor.

Finally Dr. Goodson got a question in to her because she answered. "How many?" she repeated. "Seven. Oh, Doctor."

Then her voice dropped a little. "Yes, yes. Thanks." She set down the phone and collapsed into a chair without a word.

"What did he say?" Dad asked, still piling on the soda.

"If he's still alive, he's all right," she reported. Then her mouth flew open. "You don't suppose any of the others are allergic to bee stings, do you?"

After that we counted the kids. Chester had one ear the size of a sweet potato, but he was breathing. Amy wouldn't come to the door, though Bradford told us she was ugly but alive.

She yelled something to him and he stuck his head back inside for a minute. When he appeared again, he was laughing.

"She said to tell you she had planned to bake a box cake for your stupid party but now you should forget it."

Zach was sitting on his front steps with little piles of soda all over his skin. He was petting his guinea pig and watching the puddles that the hose had left in the street when the bees attacked. The bees that had been caught in the spray hadn't drowned. They were crawling out and airing their wings a while before bumbling off.

The woman who owned the bees called Dad and told him that Amy had broken the windshield wiper on her car and if we didn't pay for a new one, she would be forced to sue.

"How much does one of those things cost?" I asked Dad.

"How much do you have?"

I handed him all our money and he frowned at it a minute. Then he patted my arm between the smudges of wet soda. "I'll make up the difference. Call it my birthday present for Chester's brother."

"Jefferson," I reminded him.

"Sure," he nodded.

After supper I went up and sat on Chester's porch until it was time to go to the drive-in movie that is our Saturday night treat. His brothers and sisters were laughing inside the house and the bird was shouting now and then. Tui the goat came over to the fence and stood on her hind legs until we picked some grass for her to eat. She laid her ear against my cheek and then turned around and looked at me upside down between her legs.

"Tui really likes you," Chester told me.

"I like Tui," I told him. "You know, we're back at first base, and we only have three days to put this party together."

Chester had that strange look on his face.

"We all really like apple pie at our house," he said.

How do you answer a remark like that? What does liking apple pie have to do with being flat broke?

He didn't even notice I hadn't commented. "Mom and Dad figured out how to have apple pie every week. They go pick apples at the end of the season. The orchardman gives them away to get his place cleaned up.

"We had the whole back of our trunk full of apples and we kids were holding the baskets in. Just as we passed the orchard greenhouse, one of my brothers shook loose and fell out. The whole bushel of apples went rolling out with him, right into the glass of the greenhouse."

He was staring off beyond Tui as if he could still see that brother of his rolling out of the truck in a shower of apples.

"The seventeen broken windows in the greenhouse cost more than the apples would have. Since then, only Eleanor and I go with them to pick apples."

"One of the kids," I repeated.

"One of my brothers," he said, looking at me that straight way.

"Jefferson," I guessed out loud.

He was still nodding thoughtfully when Dad honked out in front and I ran to get into the car.

Sunday

When I think of all the scientists who have stood around in white smocks inventing systems like radar and sonar and X ray, I have to laugh.

They could have just hired Mom.

She has some kind of extrasensory perception that can be scary.

I have been fluffing up marshmallow bags to make them look fuller than they are ever since I could open the pantry door. I've never gotten away with it once.

"If you wanted five marshmallows, why didn't you ask me?"

It's uncanny how a handful of potato chips can turn into a federal case. Would you believe that an otherwise perfectly normal lady would have memorized how many chocolate chips come in a cellophane bag?

So I should have known she would miss that little lump of ground raw beef.

She stared at the package in disbelief. "Jamie?" she asked in that tone she uses when she suspects I am running a fever.

"It was only a little wad," I told her.

She was staring at me. "Has this birthday party really gotten to you? What in the world are you going to do with a lump of raw ground beef?"

"I am going up to Chester's house," I told her.

It wasn't much of an explanation, but I was in a hurry. I was taking my wagon there to bring down the toys Chester was giving to the garage sale. As I went through the kitchen with my orange crate, I heard Mom and Dad still playing twenty questions with each other about that ground beef.

"Manx cats could eat raw beef," Dad suggested.

There was no point in my spoiling their coffee break like that.

"Try a South American swimmer," I called back.

"Yuck, oh, yuck!" Mom cried. That's an expression that she learned from me. She only uses it when she thinks about the piranhas that swim around the tank at Chester's house. They are always looking at me through the glass with a hungry expression. I like to feed them to remind myself to be careful around that tank.

Chester's house is the ugly duckling of our street. The house really belongs to the Owenses, and Chester's family only rents it. I always wondered why Chester and his family didn't paint it up nice anyway, even if it wasn't their own. Now I understand.

If I had to make a choice between having pets and making fudge and sending someone as excellent as Eleanor off to camp or painting, I'd just wait for the Owenses to paint their own house too.

And what that house lacks in looks, it makes up for in other ways.

Tui the goat waved that brush of a tail and bleated at me as I passed her fence. She might have followed me clear to the porch if a yellow ball hadn't streaked by her. She was off like a shot chasing that ball.

I stopped to watch. Tui's the only goat I ever heard of who thinks she is a dog. I imagine it started because she and Billybub, Jefferson's Dingo dog, are such good friends.

Tui chases cars and generally catches them. If she's in a good mood, she'll sit when you tell her to. And of course she chases balls and brings them back, just as Billybub does.

She was gaining on Billybub but lost at the end because that Dingo dog is so good at cornering. Then Billybub dropped the ball at the foot of the boy who had thrown it.

"Hi," he said when he saw me watching. "Chester's inside."

I nodded and watched him throw the ball again. Both Tui and the dog shot after it. But that dog is no dummy. He ran sideways like a crab to keep from turning his back on Tui. It isn't that Tui is mean. It's more that she sees the back of anyone as an invitation to send that person flying.

There's always a good humming from inside Chester's house. Kids are always talking and maybe someone is blowing a horn. Because neither of the babies was crying, I could hear the mynah bird chattering away inside.

Chester says it knows a lot of words, but mostly it repeats things that it hears all the time.

"My turn," it was yelling.

"More, please."

"I didn't do it."

I drew a deep breath as Chester came to the door.

"What smells so good?" I asked him.

"Fudge," Chester explained. "We voted on dessert and fudge won over cake. It's more exciting."

I like fudge as well as the next kid, maybe even better, but exciting?

At my puzzlement, Chester explained. "You know you'll get two of something. But until the last minute, you don't know if it will be spoonfuls or cut pieces."

I nodded. Fudge is like that at our house too.

I showed him the lump of meat I had brought for the piranhas.

"Hey," Chester said, "that was nice of you." He called James, and we went in to feed the fish. The tank is in the living room. I guess it is the living room. Chester's father's chair is in there, with a rocking chair and a footstool for his mother. Then there are a lot of places for kids to sit. In the corner are two tables with holes in the middle to stuff babies into.

The shades had been drawn against the sun and it was dark in there. The fish tank has tubes leading into it. Air bubbles stir around in green stuff, making it spooky under the little light.

I was still getting used to the dimness when James took the lid off the tank.

"Here, King," he called.

I looked into the tank. There was only one fish there, and it was a lot bigger than I remembered from before.

"Where are the other two?" I asked.

James looked at Chester as if for help.

Chester formed the word "Eaten" silently with his mouth. I figured James was still a little upset about that.

"How do you know this one is King?" I asked.

"How do you think he got his name?" James said,

wiggling the meat back and forth above the water.

The fish was watching very carefully. Trouble was, I couldn't tell whether he was watching the meat or James's finger.

When King started for the surface of the water, James dropped the meat and put the lid back on fast. Even before the glass clinked into place, the meat was gone. King didn't so much eat it as breathe it in. Then he switched over to stare at me.

"Yeah," Chester agreed, backing away too. "You're welcome, King. You're really welcome."

"Welcome, welcome, welcome," the mynah bird shouted from the kitchen where somebody had begun beating the fudge.

Chester carried a lawn bowling set out to the wagon along with some boxed games that looked brand new.

"Games only work at our house if six or more can play," he explained.

The sale was clearly going to be a success. There were cars parked on both sides of the street down by the open garage door.

Chester and I rang Amy's bell and this time she answered. She was wearing a red ski mask so that only her eyes showed. When she saw who it was, she began to cry.

"I'm through, I tell you, really through. Under this thing I look like a sack of potatoes and onions and apples all bundled in together. With hair growing on it," she added. "I don't care what happens to that old birthday party."

"It's Jefferson's birthday party," Chester reminded her. She only wailed and slammed the door hard.

"Girls care a lot about how they look," Chester said as we went on down the street. Chester's sweet potato ear had shrunk a little overnight but was still pretty colorful.

Edie was already set up with her things at the garage sale. The people were milling around looking at them and smiling at Edie. She was dressed up with her hair piled on top of her head and pulled so tight that it looked as if the roots would hurt. She had packages of bubble bath and an unopened game of pick-up sticks and a doll with a whole bunch of fancy outfits with shoes to match.

Zach had brought some puzzles, and sandwich bags full of toy wild animals separated by species. He also had printed a sign that read:

ASK TO SEE THE PUPPIES.
MISSILEANEOUS BREED
PAPER TRAINED

Zach was wearing that blue shirt with the special hole in the pocket for his rat's tail. His rat was peering out the top of the pocket with his tail hanging down comfortable and not all bunched up.

Some grownups like to tease kids. A man came walking in with his wife. He laughed at Zach's sign and punched his wife in the ribs a little.

"Hey," he said. "Look at that. Space age dogs."

"That means that I'm not sure about the breed," Zach explained. Zach is not nearly as good at spelling as he is at math.

The man winked broadly at his wife. "I'd like to see one of those out-of-this-world dogs."

The owner who was holding the garage sale looked nervous.

"You could go look through the boy's fence," he suggested.

"Maybe the dog is out to launch," the man said, jabbing his wife again.

Zach really dragged, going up to his house to get the puppy. He walked like a boy who didn't want that man to buy his dog.

Edie sold three doll dresses and made change out of a folding purse. A man who looked like a grandfather bought Chester's lawn bowling set.

New cars had pulled in by the time Zach carried the puppy down the hill. One car brought a lot of very dressed-up ladies wearing beads and smelling like a department store. They were picking up dishes and reading what was written on the bottoms.

The man reached for the puppy. "Let me see that little astronaut," he said.

"I'll just turn him around so you can see," Zach said, hanging onto his dog.

"Okay, son," the man said. "Put him down on the floor where I can see him."

Zach set the puppy on the cement floor. Those puppies are used either to grass or the rug in their doghouse. The puppy looked up and whimpered, his legs splaying out at the sides.

When Zach leaned over to pat him, the rat slid out of his pocket and hit the cement with a squeal.

Well, the puppy forgot about how strange the floor felt when that rat shot past him. The ladies also forgot what was written on the bottoms of the plates. They threw those plates every which way, shouting, "Rats. Rats."

Zach was down there under the table trying to catch the rat and the puppy. The ladies were dancing all over each other, trying to get out to their car. The man who had started it all just stood there laughing. I wished that puppy had more than milk teeth. It would have been a great time for him to learn to use them.

Chester and I apologized while we swept up the mess. The owner of the house watched us with his teeth showing but he was not smiling. I guess his wife felt worse about our ruining their sale because she was crying.

When Zach caught his animals he just walked off, leaving us to bring his toys and sign along. Edie had screamed worse than any of the ladies and shot off home, so we had to collect her stuff too.

Because we wanted to be good sports, we offered the man all the money we had made.

He must have wanted to be a good sport too because he took it and put it into his pocket.

Then he made a little speech without ever taking his teeth apart from each other.

"The moving van is coming Wednesday," he said. "I don't even want to see you kids walk past my house between now and then."

"But we need to go to school," I told him.

"Indeed you do," he agreed. "But you'll be safer if you walk on the opposite side of the street."

Chester and I went back up the hill faster than we had come down. As Chester walked along he kept putting his hand on his bee-stung ear as if to cool it.

When we had all the stuff put away in my garage, we went out and looked down the street. A whole new set of cars had come to the sale and people were walking out with things they'd bought.

"Once when we were moving we had a garage sale," Chester said dreamily. "Mom and us kids sold all this stuff on the lawn while Dad tore the truck down to be ready to travel in. When the sale was over, Eleanor gave Dad fifteen dollars and I had collected ten. Then one of the kids handed Dad a fifty-dollar bill."

He fell silent for a minute. "Dad only found out

what had been sold when he tried to put the motor back in the truck."

I stared at him.

"One of the kids sold the motor of your truck for fifty dollars!"

"What does a little kid know about the value of a motor?" Chester asked, almost defensively. "It was just sitting out there."

"Do I want to know which kid that was?" I asked him.

"Probably not," he concluded. "Probably you'd rather not know."

Monday

Usually we all go down the hill to school in a bunch. That Monday was different. Edie and Amy had already started ahead when Chester stopped by for me.

From the back Amy looked strange. When we were in class I saw that she had changed her hair. Her bangs always hang down almost in her eyes. They seemed even longer than usual. Most of the time she divides the rest of her hair in two wads. She ties these up high with ribbons to keep from being scalped by some grabby little brother or sister.

That day her hair was down. She had pulled it forward over her face as far as it would go to hide her bee stings. She looked a little like a fox peeking out of a bush.

Edie's hair was as usual but she was walking with her back stiff. I know that mad walk of hers. When she's marching along like a wooden soldier in a skirt, anything you say is a declaration of war.

Chester and I caught up with George right away. He pretended he couldn't see us. Since he was making a big thing of limping along as if he needed a crutch, we finally walked on by ourselves.

His leg apparently felt better right away because he managed to get to class before the tardy bell. Which is more than I can say for Zach.

You would have thought the janitor had put itching powder in all our seats. Nobody could sit still. There was a lot of that loud yawning that people do when a teacher isn't looking their way.

"I don't like the last few days of school any better than you do," Miss Button finally snapped. "But we are all in this together."

When everybody stared at her without shaping up, she leaned over her desk. "All right," she said. "What kind of a sentence was that? Buford?"

Poor Buford nearly jumped out of his overalls. "What kind of a what was what?" he asked.

She had to rap the ruler on the desk to quiet us down. At least she had our attention.

She got up and wrote it on the board.

We are all in this together.

The chalk hit the board like a shot when she made the period.

Buford tugged his lip inside his mouth and thought

hard. "Declaratory?" he asked in a little squeaky voice.

"Right," she told him. "Now, class, what kind of a statement is this?"

She wrote SHAPE UP on the board in giant letters, and a dozen hands started pumping the air.

Abbie with the skinny legs and braces got to answer.

"That's an imperative sentence," she said.

"And a warning," Miss Button added. "Now, open your books to page one-forty-six and sit still while Kevin starts reading."

I read after Kevin, and she went down the rows in order. I held my book and pretended to read while I looked out of the window with the corners of my eyes.

It occurred to me that those ancient Egyptians that walk sideways in our history book couldn't do what I was doing. In all those drawings they have those big noses that go straight up into their foreheads without any little dip between their eyes. When they looked sideways like I was doing, they must have only seen that big chunk of extra face with one eye.

Miss Button interrupted the reading to ask if I had lost something on my nose or was I just having trouble keeping my eyes together.

I didn't really need to look out the window anyway. I was just thinking about the other times when all of us had been broken up the way we were now.

That first week that Chester came, every single kid got mad at him. If his goat Tui hadn't run away and ended up getting our worst enemy off the streets, we might still not be friends.

Then there was the time that the great Pogo Lambert came back to visit Millard C. Fillmore, his old school. We had so many fights over that float for field day that we could never have gotten made up again if Chester's sister Eleanor and his goat hadn't made us a huge success on live TV.

I sighed. Luckily the bell rang at the same minute or Miss Button might have said something about that too.

There wasn't any way that even Tui could save us this time. She might be able to chase cars and scare somebody to death when he has his back to her but she wasn't apt to pluck us a big mouthful of nice green money for Jefferson's party.

Discouragement must have shown in my face because Zach tried to cheer me up in the lunchroom.

"Tonight we'll get that whole ten dollars from Prescott's Five and Dime. It's surefire."

I had thought the car wash and the garage sale were surefire too, so I only nodded.

After school we stood outside Prescott's window for a long time, just studying that bowl of jelly beans. Mom was right. The top layer had been faded from the sun and was dusty looking. The sign looked a little tired, too. There were suspicious spots along the edges as if a fly had rested there. In big letters, the sign said:

WIN TEN DOLLARS:
GUESS HOW MANY BEANS ARE IN THIS BOWL.
IF YOU GUESS WITHIN FIVE BEANS,
YOU ARE THE LUCKY WINNER!

"I'd feel better about this if the beans looked younger," I told Zach.

He scoffed at me. "What's your problem? Are they wrinkled? Do they have white hair?" Then he lowered his voice. "Now here's the plan." He outlined it in a careful whisper and led us inside.

Zach had borrowed thirty-five cents from his next week's allowance. While he spent it on a sack of jelly beans, Chester and I drifted over to stare at the bean bowl.

When we got back outside, Zach turned to us. "Did you get it?" he asked. "Did you get the size of the bowl?"

Chester nodded. "It's two-and-a-half hands long, one-hand deep to that last knuckle, and a hand-and-a-half high."

"Surefire," Zach said. "On to Gremlings."

Gremlings is that kind of store that you should

never go into with your mother, your father, or Zach Lund.

It's the kind of store that starts fights. Mom heads straight for the potted plants and Dad hits the ceiling.

"Forty dollars for that big weed?"

Dad goes back where the snowblowers and lawn tools are and comes up with a tube thing on a handle.

"To plant six tulips you bought that?" Mom challenges him.

Zach is the worst because they have a big pet department. He not only looks at every bird, fish, and lizard they have, he examines them as if he already were a veterinarian.

We were barely inside the door before Zach gasped, "Ferrets," and disappeared behind the rabbit cages.

"Forget him," I told Chester while we found the fishbowls.

The bowls were all sizes. They had those teeny ones that you get one pale fish in when a store has a Grand Opening. They got bigger and bigger until they jumped to fish tanks like the one King lives in.

Chester laid his hands across two or three of them before a nervous young man came over and asked if he could help.

Chester showed him a bowl the size of the one in Prescott's window and asked what size it was.

"The man turned it over and said, "Six.""

"Six what?" Chester asked.

"It's just marked six," the man replied.

"Are you sure that doesn't mean six dollars?" Chester asked. "I wanted to know how much it holds."

The man sighed and went away, carrying the bowl. A lot of clerks would rather not wait on kids. He came back and said, "It holds two gallons and it costs six dollars." He had that kind of expression that dares you to say anything more.

"Thanks a lot," Chester said. The clerk was still holding the bowl and staring after Chester when we went over to take Zach away from the ferret cage. The ferret in it knew he had a live prospect there and was running around inside a wire tube making eyes at Zach.

"Two gallons," Chester kept repeating to himself all the way to Zach's house. "That is a two-gallon bowl."

"Like a cowboy hat," Zach said.

"Those are ten gallon," I corrected him.

"Two gallon, two gallon, two gallon," Chester repeated really fast before I could confuse him.

I have to admit that Zach's idea was scientific. We measured the jelly beans. They filled one cup with seventeen left over. We each ate five and Zach got the two extra because it was his allowance we had used to buy them. When we counted, there were seventy-eight jelly beans in a cup.

Zach's idea was to find out how many jelly beans it took to fill a cup. Then we would fill a two-gallon container with something that had the same number of things to a cup. Then we would count all those things and win the ten dollars and the dusty jelly beans too.

It wasn't easy to find something that had the same number of them to a cup as the jelly beans did. Those little spotted beans were too small. We worked our way clear through Mrs. Lund's cupboard before we went to my house to look in Mom's cupboard.

She had white beans the same size as the spotted ones.

"How about kidney beans," she asked as she handed down a canister. "What do you want with them?"

"We need to count them," Chester told her, nodding in that way that indicated she would understand.

She didn't. She just sat there across the table with her chin on her hands and watched us count beans.

"That's it," Zach cried. "That's exactly it. Now," he said, turning to Mom briskly. "Do you have a container that holds two gallons?"

When she came back from the pantry she was shaking her head. "I have two one-gallon jars. Will they do?"

We looked at each other and decided they would.

"Now, do you have enough of these red beans to fill those two jars?" Zach asked her.

For a minute she looked stunned. Then she laughed. "Why would I have two gallons of red kidney beans? That would make chili for an army. And maybe a navy."

Zach's expression turned to tragic.

She sat back down by us. "I'm sorry I laughed. It's just that . . ." She started to laugh again and caught herself. "Can you explain this to me, carefully?"

"Well," Zach began. "There were eighty-seven jelly beans in the cup."

"Seventy-eight," Chester corrected him. They looked at each other and then at me.

I shrugged. I hadn't tried to remember. I had just eaten my five jelly beans and wished they were ten.

"It doesn't matter." Zach shrugged. "We can always go back to my house and count them again."

Then he explained to Mom that we needed to fill a two-gallon jar or bowl with anything the same size as the jelly beans and count them. Then we would know how many beans were in Mr. Prescott's fishbowl.

She was shaking her head. "You don't have to have beans to do that." She reached for her grocery pad with the pencil it's worth your life to take off that string.

"There are four cups to a quart," she told Zach. "Then there are four quarts to a gallon. So two gallons would be—"

Zach didn't even let her finish. He had already done it in his head. "Thirty-two cups," he shouted, all excited again.

"Your mom's a genius," Zach told me as we started out the door.

"She caught it from me," I told him, winking back at her.

You remember how we put those beans back into the sack at Zach's house?

You surely remember that Zach's house is nothing more than a walking, squeaking, tweeting, barking, mewing zoo.

We finally found the sack in the corner of the family room. Zach's rat was there beside it. He hardly even looked like a rat. He looked more like a little white watermelon with four legs and a tail.

Zach just sighed. "I know for certain that there were eighty-seven jelly beans in that cup."

Chester was quietly shaking his head.

There was nothing to do but use eighty-two, which was halfway between. Zach multiplied that by thirty-two and checked his arithmetic about five times before he called Mr. Prescott.

While he was making the call, a funny noise began in the family room, and Mrs. Lund let out a yell.

"Quick, Zach," she said. "Quick."

Zach handed me the phone and took off.

Mr. Prescott was just as jolly as anyone could be. "Zach Lund," he said as if he were really impressed. "That's the closest anyone has ever come in all these years. But sorry, son, you're more than five beans off. One try to a customer," he added. "But my, that was a good try."

Zach kept flying in and out of the kitchen to wet a cloth. Chester and I just waited.

The third time Zach came back, he was carrying his pet rat in the damp cloth. That poor rat looked awful. Even his whiskers were limp.

"That shows you what kind of jelly beans the Prescott Five and Dime has," Zach said hotly. "I'll be lucky to pull him through this."

Neither Chester nor I said anything.

That's the first time I ever saw Zach act like my mom. When she's scared, she gets mad. Zach began yelling at us because he was so afraid for his rat.

"This was a surefire thing and you blew it," he yelled. "All that work and my allowance gone and you gave him the wrong number. I mean I am so sick of this party that I could yell."

We didn't point out that he already was yelling.

Chester and I were almost out the door when the rat started gasping and began to be sick again.

"Mom was going to send enough potato chips for the whole party but now I'm not even coming. So there."

Chester and I walked to the corner of the house and stood there under the bird feeder. All the birds were gone except one fat sparrow that was bouncing along the rim of the feeder looking for something left over from winter.

Until I knew Zach's canary, Tweet, I thought that if you ate like a bird, you weren't very hungry. That's not what that expression means. To eat like a bird is to clack around a lot and throw most of your food onto the floor.

The wild birds are as bad as Tweet is. The seeds they drop from that feeder come up in the strangest weeds.

One year a sunflower came up. It got almost to the drainspout before George accidentally hit it in the neck with a baseball.

"Maybe we should give up," Chester said. "There's only tomorrow left to make money. Jefferson doesn't know about the party, so he won't be disappointed."

I stood there scrubbing my feet in those weeds. It isn't that I'm so crazy about winning. It's just that I really hate to lose. If we had been doing something totally selfish, it would have been different. To try to do something nice and have the whole entire world against us made me mad.

"Hey," Chester said. "Look at that. Look at what you have your foot on."

For a minute I just saw clover. But no. It was a whole entire clump of clovers and every one of them had four leaves.

Chester was down picking some of them and pressing them against his finger.

"Do you believe in lucky charms like this?" he asked me.

I pulled the rabbit's foot out of my pocket and showed it to him. "I've been carrying this since Saturday," I told him.

He got to his feet in a tired way.

"Like I said, we should probably give up the whole

idea. It's not our lucky week or something."

"No," I said, louder than I meant to. "We have one more whole afternoon. I'd hate to give up with a day left."

"Nobody could call you a quitter now," he told me.

"I don't care who calls me a quitter," I told him "I just care about feeling like a quitter."

We shook hands solemnly as if we were starting a club and headed up the hill.

I was telling him how well cold-drink stands always go over but he wasn't even listening.

"It's really easy to count things off and make a mistake," Chester told me, obviously still thinking about those jelly beans. "Once my dad's family had a reunion and my uncles and aunts came from all over. Dad parked our truck in the same lot where my uncles parked theirs. Since all the trucks were about alike, Dad told us to be sure to remember that ours was the third one from the end."

Already I was deciding I didn't like this story and he had barely started telling it.

I was wrong. The story was almost over.

"One of the kids got sleepy and crawled up in the back of the truck for a nap. The trouble was, he counted wrong. Dad had to drive clear to Peoria, Illinois, to bring him back home."

He didn't tell me which of his brothers this was, and I didn't ask him. I only wished I had picked some of those four-leaf clovers for myself. A little extra luck never hurt anybody.

Tuesday

You have heard about putting all your eggs in one basket. Chester and I were pouring all our hopes into one little cold-drink cooler.

Mom must have understood. She didn't say anything when I fished the paper cups out of the picnic basket. Only when I took the folding card table out of the front hall did she look concerned.

"That's never been very sturdy since . . ." When her voice trailed off I decided she really was feeling sorry for us. Any other time she would have finished that sentence with a glowing description of the time I came flying in the front door without realizing she had waxed the hall for guests.

What is amazing about that slide I took through her bridge party is that two years later she can still remember the exact cards in that winning hand she was holding. Dad says it doesn't amaze him at all and that is why he never plays as her partner.

"We're only going to put some glasses and a pitcher on it," I told her.

She nodded but still looked doubtful.

Chester brought two packages of soft-drink powder from his house and we had three. His were grape and orange. I had one strawberry and two lime.

"One package doesn't make very much, even to start with." Chester said.

"I can't stand green," I told him. "That's the only color we have two of."

"What do you think of mixing them all together for a mystery punch?" he asked.

"Sometimes they give you a mixed fruit jelly in restaurants," I remembered out loud.

"What does it taste like?"

"Sweet," I told him.

"Do people complain?"

"I never heard anybody complain," I admitted.

"Then let's mix them and make it really sweet."

We put three trays of ice cubes in the bottom of the cooler. Then we mixed the powders together and added sugar.

"The color is mysterious too," Chester said.

That color wasn't mysterious, it was repulsive. It

looked like those puddles left when snow has finally melted down. We looked at it without being able to face each other.

Somebody had to taste it. We drew straws and I lost.

"Believe it or not, it's really good," I told him.

He took a little cup. "We may have made a break-through," he admitted. "If we could just do something about that awful color."

Mom had lost interest and wandered off. I got a chair and went through the shelf where she keeps her cookie-decorating things. The bottles of green and yellow coloring had dried up but there was nearly half a bottle of the red left.

We poured all the red coloring in and then rinsed the bottle and poured that in too. It wasn't really red but a dark winish color.

"That's no more than half bad," Chester said. We tasted it again before taking it out to the table. We decided people wouldn't see it so well in the cooler so we didn't use a pitcher at all.

I had lettered the sign to read: COLD DRINK 5¢.

I turned it over and changed it to: MYSTERY DRINK 5¢.

We settled down at each end of the table to wait for business.

That street has never been so quiet in its history. Zach's cat came around and sat on the front porch to wash her face. You could hear the clank of the chains on the swings in Amy's back yard. A red bird over in the direction of the park started asking the same question over and over.

When Mom came to the door we called out to her.

"Delicious mystery drink for sale here."

After she looked in the cooler she offered to buy each of us a glass. That dime sure looked lonesome in our cigar box.

"What color is my tongue?" I asked, sticking it out at Chester.

"Very, very red," he told me.

"That's what color you are all around your mouth," I pointed out. He rubbed at his face a long time with his shirt tail. The cloth turned pink but his face didn't fade at all.

The paper boy came by and bought a glass.

"How does it taste?" Chester asked him.

"Sweet and cold," he told us, handing me another nickel for a second glass.

He rode away not knowing that he had a red clown mouth stained on his face just like Chester's.

The rule about soft-drink stands in our neighborhood is that you have to take them down when fathers start coming home for the evening.

All the sounds of late afternoon were starting. The woman next door with the apple tree changed her radio from music to news. The creak of swings from Amy's back yard stopped. The kids were all inside flattening their noses against the front window and staring at Chester and me. Zach was out feeding his pups. You knew when he set the food down because the yapping stopped in an instant. George had come out to throw his basketball through the loop on his garage. I knew he was sneaking looks at us but I didn't catch him at it.

Edie came out on her porch with her doll and began to dress and undress it from a shoebox full of clothes. The man whose blue car we had washed drove down the hill to meet his wife at the commuter train. He drove by with his nose in the air as if he couldn't see us.

Chester is the only kid in the world who wouldn't have said, "I told you so." He could have done it fairly, too. He had suggested a whole day earlier that we give up. Instead, he grinned at me and said, "At least we didn't say it was a sure thing, did we?"

Then I saw Dad's car make the turn onto our street. "We better shut up shop," I told Chester.

He looked into the cooler. "What will we do with this?"

I laughed. "What it looks like is dragon blood. Dragon blood is supposed to make things grow double their natural size."

Chester looked around our yard. "What would your mother like to have grow about ten feet tall?"

Dad was driving up the street very slowly the way all the parents do because they don't trust us kids not to run out without looking. He was looking at us and grinning. He didn't see the bicycle coming down the street until it was too late.

I knew it was one of Chester's brothers because he was coming really fast, doing wheelies every once in a while and riding with no hands.

It was Chester who found his voice. "*Jefferson*," he screamed. "LOOK OUT!"

When something very scary happens, time changes. Either time slows itself down or else I watch double time.

I saw Jefferson hear Chester.

I saw him see Dad turning that car right in the path of his bike. I saw his arms unfold as he grabbed those

90

handlebars and crouched down to see how he could miss running into Dad's car.

No one in the world could have pedaled fast enough to get around that turning car at the back. Jefferson had to make it between Dad and the garage door and he had about one split second to do that in.

I heard Dad's brakes screech and a little ping like something musical as Jefferson's bike barely nicked Dad's front fender getting by.

He had made it. Jefferson had done the most skillful bit of precision pedaling you could ask for, but he had connected with Dad's fender just enough to tumble him off the bike. The bike clattered into the bushes, and Jefferson came rolling across the lawn toward us in a sort of porcupine shape of arms and legs.

"No," Chester said quietly. "No, Jefferson, no."

It wasn't Jefferson's fault. In the choice between running *spang-whap* into Dad's car or rolling in under the legs of the folding table, he made the correct choice.

Even if that table had been sturdy it would have gone down.

There is absolutely no noise that will fill a street full of people as quick as the desperate screech of car brakes on a block where a lot of kids live.

By the time the paper cups flew all over the lawn and the cooler flipped off the table to turn upside down on Jefferson's head, the street seemed crowded.

Dad was out of his car and leaning weakly against the door. Mom was onto the porch and running for Jefferson. George's basketball was bouncing itself down the street, forgotten, while he ran toward us. Edie was yelling with a half-dressed doll clutched tight against her cheek. Zach didn't even open his gate. He came flying over the dog fence so fast that he scared his own cat up the tree next door. Amy was pushing kids back into the house, trying to get out the front door by herself.

Dad babbled as he got the cooler off Jefferson's head.

"Are you hurt, son?" he kept saying over and over like Chester's mynah bird.

Jefferson shivered when he looked up. Then he shook a couple of ice cubes out of his shirt and smiled at Dad.

If he hadn't been the color of a polished red apple from the top of his head clear to his knees, he could have passed for Chester. As it was, he looked just like Chester would if you dyed him the color of cold dragon blood.

Dad took Jefferson's arm, helping him to his feet. "You're sure you're all right?" he kept insisting.

"Couldn't be better," Jefferson said. Then he looked down at himself. "Whatever this is, it's sure cold."

Mom sounded like Edie's mother, telling Chester to get Jefferson home into a hot tub before he caught pneumonia. Only as they started off, with Chester wheeling Jefferson's bike for him, did Mom call after them.

"And, Chester, have your mother put some bleach in the bath water."

Everybody was clustered around, talking all at once.

"Mom already bought those potato chips for the party," Zach said. "Since I have to bring them anyway, I might as well come."

"I've got that box cake and some powdered sugar,"

Amy said. "I'll do the cake tonight. I really want to."

Edie's mother came over by herself. She was holding herself with her own arms, her hands on her elbows. She was as white in the face as Dad. She must have made Edie stay with the baby.

"It's a miracle," she told Dad. "A miracle that little child lived to tell this tale. Those bicycles are dangerous . . . just dangerous."

She looked up the hill after Chester and Jefferson, who were almost to their house.

"Edie promised sandwiches for his party and they'll be ready," she said. "Wrapped, of course." She frowned at Amy. "You'll have that cake covered against the flies?"

"I always cover cake," Amy told her. "Otherwise the kids would finger off all the frosting."

Edie's mother shuddered a little and went off home, still holding her elbows.

"The drink mix Mom has for the party tomorrow is orange," George said. "Nothing like that stuff." Then he went off down the hill to get his ball back.

Mom was peering thoughtfully into the cooler. "I have plenty of bleach," she told herself out loud. Dad picked up the remains of the table while I gathered up the scattered cups. The cigar box was upside down with our four nickels lost in the grass.

"Well, anyway, the party is on for sure," Dad said.

He lifted the lid of the trash barrel. I put in my load and then he threw in the table. Mom was still looking at the cooler. Then she shrugged and laughed and tossed it into the trash can too with an airy little flip.

There at the back door I could smell dinner cooking. It smelled rich and spicy and Italian. I hoped it was meatballs and spaghetti with lots of that gritty light cheese. Dad held the screen door for Mom and me. Music was coming from the radio in the house next door and I heard Zach's pups start to yap, which probably meant that Mr. Lund had come home for dinner.

I was on my second plate of spaghetti before Mom mentioned the three dollars. "I guess you'll need that money for games and prizes," she said. "If so, you're welcome."

I shook my head. "I think we need to use it for a present for Jefferson, something to bring him good luck, like a horseshoe, maybe."

Dad stopped his fork in the air and stared at me. "Luck! That's the luckiest kid I ever saw in my life."

I didn't remind them of all the things that had been happening for a solid week. I just started telling them the stories Chester had told me about Jefferson's track record as a jinx.

Mom sat and listened without saying a word until I was through.

"Let me tell you about little brothers and sisters,"

she said in this very quiet voice. "If you got your Uncle Don to telling stories about when we were growing up, he would fill your head with just the same kind. Only your Uncle Don's stories would all be about me. Older brothers and sisters remember and talk about things like that because . . ." She stopped, not able to find the right word.

"They're family history," Dad put in. "Because I'm the oldest I can tell you stories about the younger kids in my family, too. Your mother is right. Because of their older brothers and sisters, the little ones live with their childhood being brought up all their lives. But I'm right, too. Jefferson is one lucky kid . . . just as lucky as I am that he managed to miss my car."

After I was in bed I heard Mom and Dad out on the screened porch talking that quiet way they do when they are repeating old family stories to each other.

Then I thought about the week just past. Jefferson didn't have anything to do with Zach's having a hole for his rat's tail in the pocket of that blue shirt. Amy getting caught on top of the car when the bees started coming couldn't be blamed on Jefferson either. As for that big scene at the garage sale, Edie had the bad luck to be growing up afraid of her own shadow, much less rats. If Edie hadn't let out that big scream, the ladies would never have panicked the way they did. As for that business about the jelly beans from Prescott's, that was just stupid. All of us knew better than to kid ourselves that we could get ten dollars for doing nothing.

Mom had mentioned games and prizes. The box of toys I had put together for the garage sale would keep us playing for hours. Then the same toys could be prizes.

I needed to think of something really special to buy for Jefferson with that three dollars. Instead I kept remembering the screech of Dad's brakes and the way Jefferson made it through that little space there with only a ping on Dad's fender.

Talk about lucky!

Wednesday

It was like old times going to school that last day. Since we were on our bikes, George didn't have to put on his big limping act. Amy's lumps had gone down enough for her to have her hair tied up the right way. She and Edie were chattering on about the food they were bringing for the party.

Amy, of course, announced the final plans.

"We'll change clothes after school and take all the things over to the park. Chester, you can get Jefferson there without his suspecting anything, can't you?"

Chester nodded. "Just tell me what time."

"One o'clock all right?" Amy asked.

Everyone nodded but Edie. "Mom wants to know what grownup will be there to see that we are all right."

"Bears, Edie?" Amy asked acidly.

"Now stop that," Edie snapped. "Mom thinks that just in case anything happens—"

"My mom is bringing a special surprise," I told them quickly. "She'll be happy to stay for the party."

My great idea must have come to me in my sleep. I woke up thinking of a whole three dollars worth of balloons filled with helium. I could just see them there in the park. Then it would seem as if Jefferson were getting a gift from every one of us. Mom and Dad liked the idea as well as I did, but I wanted it to be a surprise for everyone else.

It was close enough to bell time that we put our bikes in the rack and started toward the door. A lot of kids come early and wait on the playground. Usually they are running around out there and yelling so loud they can hardly hear the bell.

That day they were all gathered in a little shoving group, staring at something in the middle.

"What's the big attraction?" George asked, craning his neck to see.

"Probably Jefferson," Chester told him.

Then I saw that in the middle of that bunch of kids was a bright red head.

Now there are some red-headed kids at the Millard C. Fillmore Elementary School. They are sort of sprinkled through the grades to give them color. There are carroty ones, and that deep red like furniture. There's even a girl in the second grade with pink hair who wears ribbons that match it.

This wasn't red-hair red. This was red red hair. Then the group shifted a little and I could see Jefferson's face. George let out a long whistle and would have raced over there if the bell hadn't rung.

"Mom said to thank your mother for the idea about the bleach," Chester whispered to me. "It didn't work but she appreciated the suggestion."

"On his birthday," I groaned.

Chester looked at me with surprise. "Don't worry about it, Jamie. He likes it. We all do. It's a nice change."

For a long time I'd planned to grow up and drive a great big truck. I had it all figured out. I would never pass a kid without giving three long toots on the air horn. I would never carry anything in my truck but those long-horned cattle that you see on TV.

Later I decided that being an airline pilot was better. I saw myself peering through the clouds over that big bank of instruments. Behind me I could hear the stewardess telling all the passengers to relax and enjoy their drinks. She would be assuring them that Captain

Jamie had brought lots of planes in safely after the plane had lost its engine or whatever.

Looking at Chester that morning, I had a new idea. I would be one of those men who study other people. I'd start with Chester and his family. As much as I hate to dress up, I could almost see myself in a tuxedo, bowing and accepting the Nobel Prize for figuring out how much better it is if you are a good sport about everything that happens.

I can't remember when Miss Button seemed so happy. She was wearing a new dress and higher heels than usual. For a change, she was the one who was watching the clock instead of us kids doing it.

She didn't hand out our grade cards until she shook hands with each of us as we walked out the door.

"She hates to see kids cry," Zach explained. "Especially when she's the one that made them do it."

He had his envelope ripped open before we were even outside. "I made it," he said with a big deep sigh. I looked over his shoulder because his is the only grade card I ever saw that has the same number of tardy marks as there are days of school.

My grades were okay, nothing sensational, but nothing that was going to get me into a long sit-down lecture from Dad. Across the bottom Miss Button had written a single line.

"This has been an interesting year to say the least."
I was just grateful that she decided to say the least.

Mom was going to bring the bigger toys and get there with the helium balloons about two o'clock.

"You're going awfully early," she said when I started getting my stuff together.

"We need to get it all set up," I explained. "Besides, I wouldn't miss seeing Jefferson's face for anything."

I had already told her about the bleach not working. "I wouldn't want to miss that either," she said quietly.

It took about a million trips for me to load everything into the station wagon for her. Every time I went in or out, the screen door banged.

"I can't help it," I told her. "My hands are full."

She sighed and propped the screen door open.

With the screen door quiet, I could hear Chester's family truck coming down the hill. I stood there by the car feeling dismal. That would be Chester's mom taking Eleanor off to leave for camp. Even if I looked, I probably wouldn't see her there in the cab of the truck. Seeing her leave wasn't my idea of any good thing to see anyway.

After the truck passed I did look after it. It was almost all the way down the hill. I could see a footlocker bouncing around in the back of the truck even though it was tied down. The truck was making so much noise that you couldn't even hear the dog that was running along behind it barking at the tires. The truck's rattle even drowned out the yapping of Zach's pups, who were hurling themselves wildly against their fence.

"Well, there goes my summer," I told myself, turning back to load my bike basket with party stuff.

Edie had taken charge of the picnic. With George's help, she had put two tables together to make a single long one. She had unrolled some heavy plastic to cover them. She was banging along with a stapler, fastening the covering down.

"Hey, for the wind," I decided, thinking that was pretty clever.

"Squirrels have walked on these tables," she reminded me. "Squirrels are rodents."

Just as she spoke, a fat gray squirrel leaped off a nearby tree and hit that slick plastic. He looked as astonished as Edie did as he slid past her on his tail like an otter down a mud slide.

"Rodents," she shrieked, wiping away at the place he had touched.

Amy came with all of the kids but G. She pulled Forrest in a wagon with the cake between his knees. The park is the easiest place in the world to amuse those kids. Bradford and Carrie ran for the slide.

Douglas and Eliza took over the merry-go-round. Forrest settled into the sandbox to play with a bucket and shovel.

We had come awfully early.

Edie kept herself busy cleaning the table. Zach and George and I played with the Frisbees a while and then threw a ball.

At the sound of a bike on the path we all turned to shout happy birthday to Jefferson.

Chester was there alone.

"We've lost him," he told us. "We can't find Jefferson anywhere. His dog Billybub wandered off and he went out looking for him. We're still searching all over town, but I wanted you to know."

He was barely gone before Mom pulled in with the rest of the toys and the whole rear end of the station wagon filled with red balloons that were bumping against the roof of it. She set a huge covered bowl on the table. "Carrots and celery," she said, glaring at me because I'd told her that we didn't need things like that for a party.

"Where's the birthday boy?" she asked.

"His dog ran away and he's looking for him," I explained. "Now Chester and the others are looking for both him and the dog."

All of Amy's kids had gathered around the station wagon to stare at the balloons.

Edie will probably be an actress when she grows up. She was walking back and forth looking worried and clasping and unclasping her hands like her mother does. It was a great imitation, except that I'm not sure she knew she was doing it. I made a note that I could explain about Edie to the world too. Worrying is catching, like chicken pox and pink eye. Only it doesn't go away after three weeks like they do.

In about a half-hour Chester came spinning in again. Amy's kids were all hungry so they were walking around crunching on carrots and celery. Chester was all flushed in his face. There were dark places on his shirt where he had sweated through. The green sock on his left foot was hanging clear down over his laces.

"Now Tui the goat is gone," he explained. "She hates being without Billybub so she's gone too."

"Where have you looked?" Mom asked. "Maybe we could help."

"All over town," Chester said. "We even reported it to that policeman down by the school and he's looking."

Then it hit me.

"Eleanor," I cried.

"Eleanor left for camp a long time ago," Chester told me.

"But how did she leave?" I asked. I saw that scene again as if it were a not-so-instant replay. I was at the garage door looking down the street. Zach's pups were hurling themselves against the fence. The footlocker was in the back of the truck, and there was a dog running behind the truck, barking at the tires.

"The bus," Chester said.

"That's where the dog went," I told him.

Chester and Mom stared at each other. Our bus station is way out on the edge of town where nobody ever would go except to take a bus.

Mom left the balloons with me to have more room in the station wagon. She and Chester were out that drive within seconds.

It seemed as if they were gone forever. Maybe having five little kids trying to climb you to get to your balloons makes you lose your sense of time.

We heard the horn honking even before we could see the station wagon turning into the park. It was marvelous. There is nothing like seeing a goat sitting up in the front seat of a station wagon to make kids forget about helium balloons.

The dog Billybub was the first one out, with Chester and Jefferson right on his heels. Amy held her hands up like the music teacher and made a shrill whistle between her front teeth.

Boy, did we ever make that park ring, singing happy birthday to Jefferson.

He just stood there with his mouth open. That was the most amazed bright red boy you have ever seen in your life.

Then he grinned a nice white grin. Billybub was jumping around, giving everybody great big dog hello's as Mom opened the front door of the car.

I guess Tui didn't want to miss the fun. She came flying over Mom in one big leap. Then she began to run big goat circles around all of us. Every once in a while she'd give a leap and touch all four hooves together in midair.

Everybody was laughing, even Mom who isn't used to having goats walk over her lap.

I guess I must have been laughing my head off because I forgot something I've known ever since Chester moved to the top of the hill.

I forgot that you don't turn your back on Tui.

One minute she was rounding the end of the table and the next minute she was behind me.

It didn't really hurt.
Well, it didn't hurt much.
There for a minute I knew
how a football feels when it
is kicked for that point
after touchdown.

I forgot that I was holding
three dollars worth of
helium-filled balloons.
They were off and gone in a
second. Some of them caught
in the trees and went off
like firecrackers. Most of
them floated free, bright and
wonderful against that
blue sky.

It was absolutely silent there
for a moment as we all stared up
at the whole sky filled with Jefferson's
bright red birthday balloons.

Jefferson still hadn't moved when I glanced over at him. He was staring up with the most wonderful smile on his face. Then he was whispering, as if he were afraid his words might make the wonder of those balloons go away. "The whole sky
full of red balloons,"
he was saying.
"Birthday balloons.
My birthday balloons."

Just then the rest of Chester's family came scooting down the path. Right in the middle of all those bicycles and tricycles was a police car, scrunching a little on the gravel as it pulled in beside Mom's station wagon.

The officer who got out was the one who works over by our school. He hitched his trousers and came toward us, grinning.

"This is a surprise party," George told him.

"So I heard." Then he looked around and nodded at Jefferson.

"You must be Jefferson," he said, grinning.

Not Chester's brother, not Eleanor's brother, but just Jefferson.

"Happy birthday, Jefferson," he said. "When we saw those balloons, the kids and I figured you'd found the runaways."

"At the bus station out at the edge of town," Chester explained.

"We have lovely sandwiches," Edie said. "Won't you join us?"

He looked around at all of us. "That's mighty kind of you but I need to make a report. I need to call off the search for a bright red boy, a yellow goat, and a spotted dog. There're probably other things we police need to get to today."

He reached out his hand to Jefferson. When he saw the color of Jefferson's hand, he hesitated but shook it anyway.

"Happy birthday, Jefferson," he said again. "I'd say that you are one lucky kid."

When he took his hand back he wiped it on his pants, just in case.

About the Author

MARY FRANCIS SHURA has written over twenty books for young people. Born in Kansas, not far from Dodge City, the author has lived in many parts of the United States, including California and Massachusetts. Both of her parents came from early settler families of Missouri.

Aside from writing fiction for young readers and adults, Mary Francis Shura enjoys tennis, chess, reading, and cooking—especially making bread.

The author is married and the mother of a son, Dan, and three daughters, Minka, Ali, and Shay. She currently makes her home in the western suburbs of Chicago, in the village of Willowbrook.

About the Artist

SUSAN SWAN was born in Coral Gables and received the degree of M.F.A. with Honors from Florida State University. She has illustrated text and trade books, and lives in Westport, Connecticut.